Sir Quinton Quest Hunts the Yeti

Kaye Umansky and Judy Brown

Collins

Look out for more *Jumbo Jets* from Collins

Finlay MacTrebble and the Fantastic Fertiliser • **Scoular Anderson**

Forecast of Fear • **Keith Brumpton**

Trouble on the Day • **Norma Clarke**

The Curse of Brian's Brick • **James Andrew Hall**

Invasion of the Dinner Ladies • *Pickles Sniffs it Out* • **Michaela Morgan**

We Won the Lottery • **Shoo Rayner**

Bernie Works a Miracle • **Leon Rosselson**

Charlie and Biff • *Fergus the Forgetful* • *Fidgety Felix* •

Queen Lizzie Rules OK • **Margaret Ryan**

My Mum • **Dee Shulman**

The Man in Shades • *Talking Pictures* • **Pat Thomson**

Sir Quinton Quest Hunts the Yeti • *Sir Quinton Quest Hunts the Jewel* •

Kaye Umansky

Gosh Look Teddy, it's a Werewolf • **Bob Wilson**

The Baked Bean Cure • *Dad's Dodgy Lodger* • **Philip Wooderson**

First published by A & C Black Ltd in 1992
Published by Collins in 1993
10 9 8 7 6 5
Collins is an imprint of HarperCollins*Publishers*Ltd,
77–85 Fulham Palace Road, Hammersmith, London W6 8JB

ISBN 0 00 674500 8

Text © Kaye Umansky 1992
Illustrations © Judy Brown 1992

The author and the illustrator assert the moral right to
be identified as the author and the illustrator of the work.
A CIP record for this title is available from the British Library.

Printed and bound in Great Britain by
Omnia Books Ltd, Glasgow

Hello there! I am Sir Quinton Quest, the world famous explorer. You've heard of me, of course. Who hasn't?

Exploring has always been my passion. Even as a small baby, no play pen could hold me. Yes, I certainly displayed my roving spirit at an early age. I think I can truthfully say I crawled where no baby has ever crawled before.

See this? One of my proudest possessions. Explorer Of The Year Challenge Cup, presented by SOFE (Society Of Famous Explorers, of which I am a proud member). Not to be confused with Sofe the tea lady, ha ha.

I've won this delightful cup five years running. That's a record. All the other explorers are jolly green with envy, but as I always point out, it's no more than I deserve. When it comes to exploring, I'm your man.

This is Muggins, my butler. I take him with me on all my little jaunts. He loves exploring. Wouldn't miss an expedition for anything.

You rang, Sir?

We're off on another expedition, Muggins.

Very good, Sir.

Oh no, no, anything but that!

This is Lady Cynthia Quest, my good wife.

She prefers to stay at home.

But enough of them. You'll be wanting to hear about my famous Yeti quest. In some ways, it turned out to be one of my most interesting expeditions, although of course I never did see hide nor hair of a Yeti. Not that I ever expected to, of course.

It all began one morning when I picked up the *Daily Explorer*. I have always taken the *Explorer*. I write a lot of complaining letters to it.

Dear Sir,

I really must protest about the fact that free figgy biscuits are no longer provided with tea at the Explorer's Club. This is truly an outrage.

Yours sincerely,

Sir Quinton Quest (Explorer Of The Year Five Times Running)

Also, it's got a nice easy crossword.

Across

2. Sharp instrument used by explorers to cut a jungle path.
3. What explorers prefer not to do when up a mountain.

Down

1. What explorers like to do.
4. Used by explorers for drinking soup.

Besides, I enjoy reading Tip Of The Week. In fact, I've sent in several Tips Of The Week myself. Had several published, too. One of my better ones was "Save On Huskies. Take Your Butler". Many people have since thanked me for that. However, when I opened the *Explorer* on this particular morning, little did I know what awaited me . . .

The Daily Explorer

SCOOP! THE YETI EXISTS!

Findley Ffoothold, that up and coming, popular young explorer, has recently returned from the Himalayas with astonishing new proof that the Yeti exists! Ffoothold claims that the photograph below is a GENUINE Yeti's footprint. A spokesperson from SOFE is quoted as saying "This could be enough to win young Ffoothold the coveted Explorer Of The Year Challenge Cup" blah blah . . .

Horror! The entire front page was devoted to that young upstart Findley Ffoothold – my explorer rival!

Bunkum! Balderdash! Tosh, tripe and piffle! That's what I thought about that! How dare the *Explorer* publish such rot! I almost decided then and there to cancel my subscription. (I didn't, but only because of Tip Of The Week.)

I examined the photograph carefully. ''Genuine Yeti's footprint'' indeed! That young whippersnapper Ffoothold wouldn't know a Yeti's footprint from a whale's armpit.

whale's armpit

The photograph was obviously a fake.
I knew Ffoothold. A sight too big for his
disgracefully overpriced climbing boots, if
you ask me. The young pup's ambition
knew no bounds. Why, once I even found
him sitting in MY CHAIR at the Explorer's
Club! Unbelievable!

I knew he had his eye on my Explorer Of
The Year Challenge Cup and would stop
at nothing to win it! Well, I wasn't going
to let him.

Then and there, I decided to go to the Himalayas and see for myself. If the Yeti did indeed exist, I would come back with bigger, better photographs. Probably even an interview.

If I found nothing, I would expose Ffoothold for the rotter he is. Let's face it. He's not even a proper explorer. More a trumped-up mountaineer. To be a real explorer, you need the following:

Naturally, I've got all of them. So who better than I to come up with the evidence? If, in fact, such evidence existed . . .

There was no time to be lost. The first thing I did was make a list of essential items of equipment.

List Of Essential Items

AA card (in case sleigh breaks down)

Alarm clock

Antifreeze

Aqualung (in case I have the misfortune to fall through ice)

Axe

Baked beans (NOT curried variety – tell Lady C)

Barometer

Batteries

Bed

Binoculars

Blankets (four, plus electric one)

Boots (fur-lined, make sure
          Muggins cleans them)

Boot polish

Bow-tie

Brandy (for medicinal purposes)

Brush and comb

Butterfly net

Camera (don't forget film)

Camping stove

Candles

Candelabra

Cardigans (NOT one with knitted chicken)

Cereal (Bran balls, choc flavoured)

Chicken soup

China

Chocolate (drinking and bars of)

Chronometer

Coat (warm)

Cocoa

Cologne

Compass

Cooking utensils

Cutlery

Diary

Dinner jacket (get Muggins or Lady C to press)
Dressing gown
Duvet
Electric generator
Emergency supply jelly babies (don't forget)
Essential reading material: *Deserts – Miles O'Sand*
Explorer's Guide – Ivor Mapp
Hell On Ice – Torville & Dean
Mountains – Ben Nevis
Jungles – Tarzan

Extra bow-tie (just in case I lose other one)
Film (don't forget camera)
Flag
Folding table and chair
Fridge (small)
Gramophone (don't forget records – see V)
Grappling hook
Ground Sheet
Hammock
Hankies
Headache pills
Hot water bottle
Iron
Ironing board
Kettle
Knife
Maps
Matches

Mirror
Mittens
Monocle (spare)
Moustache net
Moustache wax
Mug
Needle and thread
Oil lamp
Pen
Pencil
Pencil sharpener

Photograph of Lady Cynthia (NOT the one of her squinting)
Pitons
Pyjamas
Roll of sticky tape
Rope
Sandwiches (pref. smoked salmon. NOT cheese
and tomato)

Scarf (woolly)
Sextant
Shampoo
Shirts (clean. Muggins or Lady C to iron)
Sick pills
Skates (tell Muggins to polish)
Skis (ditto)
Sleeping bag
Sledge
Slippers

Snow shoes
Soap on rope
Socks (1 doz. prs)
Stamps
Sticks for rubbing together (in case matches get damp)
Stick for pointing at things
String (ball of)
Sunglasses (in case of snow blindness)
Swimming costume (in case plane comes down over sea)
Table-cloth
Talcum Powder
Tea bags
Telescope
Tents (one for me, one for supplies and, space permitting,
    one for Muggins)
Thermometer
Thermos flask (large)
Tins (tell Muggins to take plenty)
Toilet rolls (soft for me, hard for Muggins)
Toothbrush
Toothpaste
Torch
Towel
Tray (leave choice to Muggins)
Trouser Press
Umbrella
Vests (warm with sleeves. NOT itchy one)
Victor Sylvester gramophone records
Washing-up liquid (leave choice to Muggins)
Wine
Wine glass
Woolly hat
Woolly jumpers
Writing materials
Yeti horn (I suppose)

CHAPTER FOUR

*In which Sir Quinton plans the route,
Muggins packs and Lady Cynthia makes
a private telephone call*

I presented Muggins with my list.

He thought it a little long, but as I
explained to him, we explorers like to be
prepared. One never knows what one
might need.

I ordered Muggins to get on with the packing. I, of course, planned our route. Route planning is most important.

Lady Cynthia spent a great deal of time on the telephone booking our flight. She's always so helpful at these times. It really is jolly sporting of her. I consider myself most fortunate to have such an understanding wife.

Preparations took all day. I felt quite exhausted. I gave Muggins and Lady Cynthia their final instructions, then retired to bed, reflecting that I needed to be up bright and early the next morning.

But before I went to sleep, I wrote the title of my new journal.

I always keep diaries of my expeditions. Lady Cynthia will tell you they make fascinating reading.

The Yeti! What a strange image that word conjures up! Otherwise known as the Abominable Snowman, this elusive beast has haunted the dreams of us in the Explorer's Club for many years. Although those of us with a modicum of common sense firmly believe there is no such creature, we have all at some time or other fantasized about being the first to find one.

From time to time, reports come back of giant footprints in the snow. Young upstarts claiming to be explorers (Ffoothold, for example) claim to have fresh proof. The Explorer's Museum is awash with such so called "evidence".

Poppycock! Fakes, the lot of 'em. Make no mistake about it. If the Yeti exists, there is only one person with the right combination of cunning and experience to track it down.

CHAPTER FIVE

In which Sir Quinton breakfasts upon kippers, toast, muffins, eggs and a large pot of tea before departing for the Himalayas

As instructed, the following morning, Muggins woke me at the crack of dawn.

I thought he looked a little crumpled and red around the eyes, and told him so. If there's one thing I can't stand it's sloppiness. He informed me he'd been up all night packing.

21

Good, loyal chap – and keen as mustard.
No excuse for standards dropping,
however.

First, I took a long, hot bath – my last
chance before entering on a life of
hardship.

I then ate my breakfast and made helpful
suggestions as Muggins and Lady Cynthia
stowed the equipment into the car.

After an uneventful journey, we arrived
at the airport. There was a bit of a fuss
about the luggage, but I soon showed
them who was boss.

Muggins and I posed for a final
photograph before boarding the
aeroplane . . .

. . . and at long last, we were airborne. Lady Cynthia waved until we were out of sight. I hoped she would get the bus home all right. The poor woman misses me terribly when I go off on my little jaunts. Ah well. That's one of the penalties of being married to a world famous explorer . . .

CHAPTER SIX

In which Sir Quinton and Muggins arrive at the Himalayas and find positively no sign of the Yeti

At long last, we arrived at the foot of the Himalayas. It was cold, bitterly cold. The thermometer registered sub zero.

My monocle froze over in seconds, and Muggins put a scarf on.

The plane took off, and we were quite, quite alone. All around was the wild, frozen waste, broken only by the odd pine tree.

Off we set. I led the way, of course. As we went, I took a great many photographs of the snow, just to prove that there were POSITIVELY NO FOOTPRINTS. Muggins followed behind with the supplies. What a stout fellow he is . . .

YETI FLASH

(NOTE: *For the benefit of readers who are unfamiliar with the Yeti language, a translation has been provided*)

Hi there! Sorry interrupt. Yeti here. In Yeti language, me called Squiggle Pine Tree Wiggly Line. But you can call me Bob.

See that? Me standin' 'round mindin' own business when big iron bird fly down and coupla weirdos get out bird's tummy. Little hairy fat bossy one and tall thin one who do all work. Weirdos got lotta stuff with 'em. What for, me wonder?
What weirdos want?
Why they here?

Me decide play detective and follow. All this snow 'round, nothin' else better to do.

29

CHAPTER SEVEN

In which Sir Quinton and Muggins make camp and try their hand at waltzing

We walked all day. Soon, night fell and I ordered Muggins to make camp. This took some time, as there were the tents to erect, the fire to light, the provisions to unpack and the dinner to cook. I urged Muggins to make haste. All this exploring gives one a raging appetite.

At last my tent was up. Whilst Muggins busied himself with menial tasks, I dressed for dinner. I always dress for dinner on expeditions. It's good for morale.

After my meal, I instructed Muggins to wind the gramophone. I always like a little dance after dinner. I find it aids the digestion.

I felt much better after a bite to eat and a waltz or two. Muggins proved quite good at following my lead. I recall thinking that perhaps tomorrow night we might try the quickstep. But suddenly, the events of the day caught up with me and I was overwhelmed with exhaustion. I left Muggins to clear up and retired to my tent.

31

I regret to say that Muggins had failed me. Despite specific instructions, he had forgotten to place my pyjamas next to my hot water bottle! I made a mental note to have a word with him about that in the morning.

I was tired, darned tired. It was as much as I could do to undress myself. In fact, I called out to Muggins to come and give me a hand, but he didn't seem to hear.

Somehow, I managed it. But before I gave way to sleep, I forced myself to write up the first day's entry into my journal so that none of the fascinating details would be lost.

CHAPTER EIGHT

In which Sir Quinton's thoughts turn to home, Muggins writes a postcard and the Yeti's thoughts turn to grub

Day One

Got up at crack of dawn. Light breakfast of kippers, toast, eggs, muffins and a large pot of tea. Went to airport. Cynthia came to see me off. Touch of tummy trouble, probably all the excitement. Landed in Himalayas 15.30 hours. Everywhere snow, snow, quick, quick, snow! (Small joke). Walked in snow all day. Set a fair pace. Muggins hard pressed to keep up. As I thought, no sign of Yeti. Pitched camp. Muggins cooked dinner. Waltzed. Decided to have an early night. As I lie here in my sleeping bag, my thoughts turn to home. I wonder what Lady Cynthia is doing right now. Knitting me another cardigan? At her flower arranging class, perhaps? Organising a jumble sale? Weeping over her solitary mug of bedtime Horlicks?

Whatever it is, I'm sure she'll be thinking of me . . .

With those fond words, I closed my
journal. Outside, darkness had fallen and
a blizzard was blowing up. I hoped
Muggins had managed to erect his tent
successfully. It was going to be a wild
night. I could hear the roar of vast
avalanches in the distance.

But it takes more than a little bit of noise
to keep me awake. Unlike poor Muggins,
who tells me he is a light sleeper.

Dear Mum,
Having an awful time.
He's making me do all
the work as usual and
the tent's too small again.
Please reserve that
Careers book for me at
the library. It's v. cold
here, although I am
wearing my scarf. Outside
I can hear vast avalanches
which

MRS MUGGINS
BETHNAL GREEN
LONDON
ENGLAND

YETI FLASH

Hello. It me again. Bob. Sorry interrupt, but that no avalanche. That me roarin' in triumph! Look what me found! Grub!

Yum yum. That what we Yeti's like best. Me get stuck in.

But wait! This too good to keep to self. Me greedy, but not THAT greedy.

Me go get relations.

CHAPTER NINE

In which Bob goes to get his relations and does a comic turn

Me go to secret cave up mountain where we Yetis live. Me give relations big surprise. Me say, "Hey! What you think of outfit?"

Relations cluster round and admire. Me tell 'bout big iron bird. Relations spellbound at my charismatic performance.

When me tell about weirdos, relations die laughing. Me make real show of it. Relations think me real comedian.

Last of all, me tell relations about grub.

That do it. Relations can wait no longer.
Me lead way to weirdos camp. Me draw
veil over next bit.

CHAPTER TEN

In which disaster strikes but Sir Quinton copes brilliantly

I awoke the following morning, feeling much refreshed after a quiet, uneventful night. It was then that Muggins came hurrying into my tent. He was wild eyed and gesticulating. I guessed he had some bad news.

I was right. Disaster had struck! Wolves had got into our supply tent! All that was left was a tin of baked beans. There was nothing else for it. I would have to tighten my belt and ration myself to two beans a day – one for breakfast, one for supper. What Muggins would do for food I couldn't imagine.

Of course, there was my secret emergency supply of jelly babies, but I decided to keep quiet about those.

I didn't intend to let this set-back spoil my plans. I had come to do some serious exploring, and serious exploring was what I was going to do. After my breakfast bean, I decided what equipment I would take with me.

It is most important to select wisely, as one's very life hangs upon such things. After much deep thought, I selected the jelly babies, a map, a magnifying glass, my camera, my stick for pointing, a compass, my binoculars and a thermos of tea. And a roll of sticky-tape, of course. After some hesitation, I also took the Yeti horn.

The Yeti horn. Hmm. To my mind, a rather silly contraption which Lady Cynthia ordered as a birthday present from the Explorer's Catalogue. I must admit being rather surprised at her choice of gift, particularly as what I really wanted was a hot air balloon. Of course, I didn't say so. I didn't want to appear ungrateful. Unfortunately, Lady Cynthia does have a tendency to be taken in by advertising.

Explorers! When you next venture into the Himalayas, don't leave home without your Yeti Horn! It makes a sound which Yetis simply cannot resist. One blow, and if any Yetis are in the area, you'll know it all right!

The manufacturers claim that it makes the Yeti's love call. A likely tale! I mean, a non-existent creature can hardly have much of a love call! I didn't really want to bring it, but didn't want to hurt Lady Cynthia's feelings.

"Don't forget to try out the Yeti horn I bought you, dearest." Those were her last words to me. Then she turned and went back home alone to do some knitting or feed chicken soup to poor people or something. What a dull life the poor woman leads.

Ah well, enough of her. Back to me.

I instructed Muggins to stay behind and guard the one remaining precious tin of baked beans with his life.

Guard this tin with your life, Muggins.

I thought he looked rather glum. I offered to post his postcard for him, seeing I was going out, but he said he hadn't finished it. That'll teach me not to put myself out for the hired help in future. Feeling slightly annoyed, I left the camp.

CHAPTER ELEVEN

In which Sir Quinton has an unfortunate accident

It didn't take long before my mood lifted. This, of course, is what we intrepid explorers enjoy most. Out in the wild, alone. Facing peril fair and square. Using our wits and experience to battle with the elements. Laughing in the face of danger.

Remember what I told you an explorer needs? Brains, brawn, cool head and so on? Well, I certainly needed them now.

I boldly struck out across the white wasteland. One false step, and it could be the end of me.

But I'm an old hand at this sort of thing. I know what sort of things to avoid, and what to watch out for. This is where experience comes in useful.

As I walked, I carefully examined the snow for the slightest signs. Hair, droppings, a footprint . . . anything really. But no. Nothing. Just as I thought. I took several more rolls of film as evidence.

So intent was I on looking for footprints,
I confess I failed to notice the precipice.
A small mistake but, as it turned out,
a disastrous one.

It could have been even worse, mind.
I was lucky. My foot caught in a small
branch or something, and I dropped
harmlessly onto a ledge below. When the
blood had drained from my head and my
stomach had rejoined my body, I
scrambled back up.

It had been a frightening ordeal. But I didn't allow it to unnerve me. As all good explorers should, I kept a cool head and inspected what was left of my equipment.

There wasn't a lot of it. My map and compass had been lost down the precipice. So had my camera, my magnifying glass and my binoculars. My thermos flask was leaking tea all over my socks. However, all was not lost. I still had my jelly babies, my stick and, thank heaven, my roll of sticky tape. Oh, and the Yeti horn. Mustn't forget that.

I had intended to head back for base camp. But, having lost both map and compass, I was unsure of the direction. Yes, I was lost. But, being a true professional, I naturally knew what to do. Somehow, I must alert Muggins to my predicament.

I tried shouting, but to no avail.

I had no idea that the Yeti horn would be so loud.

I personally doubt that it was me blowing it that caused the avalanche. I still maintain it was coincidence.

However, there was a rumbling and a crashing and an unpleasant shivering sensation . . .

Then all went white and I knew no more.

Can you believe this?
Little fat weirdo
frozen solid. What
we goin' to do?

What indeed?

Beats me.

Haven't
the snowiest.

Him may
well ask.

Oh well. First things first. It lunch time
now. Time to knock off. Time to take loot
back to cave and get stuck in. We Yetis
take lunch time seriously. Important Yeti
rule: never make decision on empty
tummy. Eat first, make minds up later.

Weirdo grub delicious. Make nice change from pine needles. We all have HUGE lunch. Full tummy good thing for Yetis. It put us in good mood. It make us want to sing happy songs . . .

And dance . . .

And do cave paintings . . .

. . . and tell jokes. We Yetis happy types. We very fond of jokes.

Yes, we Yetis love good laugh. Best of all, we like practical jokes. We remember time coupla months ago when *FIRST* weirdo come. We play lotta tricks on him. That good fun.

We drop snowballs on his head.

We make HUGE footprint in snow.

We mess him about something rotten. Ho, ho, what a laugh that was. But enough of trip down Memory Lane. Me suddenly remember little fat weirdo propped up outside. It time him goin' home before he catch worse cold. Me kinda fond of him. Him very smooth and slippery. Him slide nicely. We push him off down mountain. We aim him at base camp. We Yetis dead kind-hearted, really.

CHAPTER THIRTEEN

In which Sir Quinton, against all odds,
manages to crawl back to base camp

How I ever managed to get back to base
camp I will never know. I certainly have
no memory of it. I can only assume that,
against all odds, I somehow crawled.
What an incredible feat. What a tribute to
my stamina and grit.

It is just as well I arrived when I did. Back
at base, poor Muggins was beginning to
lose his grip. When I came round from
my faint, you should have heard the
nonsense he came out with. Some cock
and bull story about being trapped in his
tent by a pack of wild animals, can you
believe? He even claims one of them ate
his postcard!

The poor chap was quite deranged. Came out with a terrible load of old drivel. Claimed I was FROZEN SOLID when I arrived back. Reckons he had to chip me out with a pick axe and thaw me in front of a fire. Me! His leader!

"Muggins," I told him kindly. "That cannot be. If I had been frozen solid, I wouldn't have been able to crawl, would I?" But the poor, deluded fellow couldn't see it. I took no notice of his wild babblings. It was obvious that he was suffering from temporary snow madness.

Needless to say, he had missed my leadership. He was pathetically pleased to see me and greatly relieved when I took charge again.

Regretfully, I decided that we must leave immediately. Our supplies were sadly depleted, and a great many essential pieces of equipment were missing, including my stick for pointing. Now, that was something I couldn't do without, particularly in my weakened state.

Besides, it was blooming cold.

CHAPTER FOURTEEN

*In which Sir Quinton and Muggins
struggle back to the plane stop and resign
themselves to a long wait*

Keep going, Muggins! Mush!

The way back was long and hard, but
somehow I managed to keep Muggins
going. Finally we reached the plane stop.
According to the timetable, there was a
plane due. Of course, as we all know, that
doesn't mean that one will actually come.
Usually you wait and wait for weeks and
weeks, then three land at once. We
settled down for a long wait. I kept myself
warm by writing
in my journal.

Muggins read
a book.

A CAREER IN LORRY DRIVING

CHAPTER FIFTEEN

In which Sir Quinton and Muggins are homeward bound

What a welcome sound! The roar of an approaching aeroplane. What's more, it wasn't full! Imagine our joy! Gleefully, we flagged it down.

We were even more delighted when we realised it was a proper one, with a charming hostess and an in-flight movie and sick bags and hot food and so forth.

I ordered lobster thermidor and
champagne for myself and a fish paste
sandwich and a small glass of weak lemon
squash for Muggins. I felt he deserved a
little something after his ordeal.

I was, of course, disappointed that our
expedition had to be cut short. I had
intended that we should be gone for at
least three weeks, and here we were
returning after only two days. However, I
soon cheered up when I thought of Lady
Cynthia, and how thrilled she would be
at my unexpected return.

She would have written to me by now, of course. A long, affectionate letter about her jam-making activities and pottery class. With any luck, I could be home before she posted it, thus giving her a lovely surprise and at the same time saving the cost of a postage stamp.

To be quite frank, I was looking forward to a quiet time being waited on in the comfort and peace of my own home. As I have said before, these expeditions can be very tiring, even for an experienced professional like myself.

Above all, though, I felt that I had done what I set out to do. I had examined the Himalayas very thoroughly, and had found not a single scrap of evidence to support that young bounder Findley Ffoothold's wild claim.

At the first opportunity, I planned to stride into the Explorer's Club and laugh in Ffoothold's face.

I would present him with my photographs of plain, smooth, mint condition snow and ask him what he thought about that!! He wouldn't like it, but that was just too bad.

Yes, I'm pretty sure the Explorer Of The Year Challenge Cup will be mine again this year. What's more, nobody can say I don't deserve it. After all, I, Sir Quinton Quest, have proved beyond any shadow of doubt that
THE YETI DOES NOT EXIST.